W9-CMU-318

Ned's Nose Is Running!

by David Michael Slater

illustrated by S.G. Brooks

magic wagon

visit us at www.abdopublishing.com

For Addison—DMS

Published by Magic Wagon, a division of the ABDO Group, 8000 West 78th Street, Edina, Minnesota 55439. Copyright © 2010 by Abdo Consulting Group, Inc. International copyrights reserved in all countries. All rights reserved. No part of this book may be reproduced in any form without written permission from the publisher.

Looking Glass Library™ is a trademark and logo of Magic Wagon.

Printed in the United States.

 Manufactured with paper containing at least 10% post-consumer waste

Text by David Michael Slater
Illustrations by S.G. Brooks
Edited by Stephanie Hedlund and Rochelle Baltzer
Interior layout and design by Becky Daum
Cover design by Becky Daum

Library of Congress Cataloging-in-Publication Data
Slater, David Michael.
 Ned's nose is running! / by David Michael Slater ; illustrated by S.G. Brooks.
    p. cm.
 Summary: When Ned has to give an oral report in health class, his nose starts running and his teacher's nose is out of joint.
 ISBN 978-1-60270-658-3 (alk. paper)
 [1. Nose—Fiction. 2. English language—Idioms—Fiction.] I. Brooks, S. G., ill. II. Title.
 PZ7.S62898Nh 2009
 [E]—dc22

                2008055341

"**Ned!** You're next," Ned's health teacher called. Ned tried to hide by putting his nose in a book.

"Don't tell me you forgot," said Mrs. Nosering. "Your name is on the calendar—it's as plain as the nose on your face."

"No, I'm ready!" Ned said before she got her nose out of joint. Mrs. Nosering was a very hard-nosed teacher. But she'd hit it on the nose: Ned *had* forgotten. He was sure he was going to pay through the nose for it, too.

"Um . . . ," Ned began.

Ned had no idea what to say. The whole class was looking down their noses at him. They could tell he forgot. What could he do?

"Ah," Ned said, scratching his nose. "I hate having a cold. I . . . um . . . I have the worst one ever right now. You wouldn't believe it! My nose won't stop ruh . . . ruh . . ."

Ah-CHOO!

Ned sneezed so hard that his nose blew right off his face.

It started running, right out of the room. Ned always did have a nose for trouble.

Ned followed his nose, but he was beaten out the door

—by a nose.

Nosy students watched from doorways as Ned chased his nose through the halls. How could he stop his nose from running?

"Keep your nose out of my stuff!"

a student yelled as Ned and Ned's nose ran
through the art room.

"Keep your nose clean!"

a teacher said as they ran through the locker room.

"No nosing around in here!"

the cook shouted as Ned's nose led him through the kitchen.

Ned's nose was heading back toward class!

Ned had to think fast. He opened the juice and spilled it on the soap.

Ned tossed the slippery soap ahead on the floor. Then he took a nosedive! Ned nosed ahead at incredible speed! He grabbed his nose and went sliding into the classroom.

Ned needed a moment, but then he was ready. He turned to his class and said, "And that's how I learned to stop a runny nose!"

"Ned! It's your turn," Mrs. Nosering cried. "Are you ready?"

"Yes!" said Ned, coming to the front of the class. "I'm going to tell a story about how I stopped my nose from running . . . all over the school."

"That sounds . . . very unusual." said Mrs. Nosering. "But stories are nothing to thumb your nose at."

"Thanks, Mrs. Nosering," said Ned. "This story will blow you away. But don't worry, I won't rub anybody's nose in it."

"Before I begin," Ned said to the class, "let me just say that's not a booger in my nose. . . . *It's snot!*" Ned continued over his classmates' laughter, "I hate having a cold. I've got the worst one ever right now . . ."

Idioms in *Ned's Nose Is Running!*

An idiom is an expression that means something different than the words would by themselves. Here are the meanings for some of the idioms in this book:

Hit it on the nose—got it exactly right
Keep your nose clean—stay out of trouble
Look down your nose—think you are better than something or
  someone
Nose out of joint—being upset
Nosing around—snooping
Pay through the nose—pay excessively for something
Plain as the nose on your face—obvious
Rub anyone's nose in it—tease someone
Took a nosedive—fell headfirst

About the Author

David Michael Slater lives and teaches seventh grade Language Arts in Portland, Oregon. He uses his talents to educate and entertain with his humorous books and informative presentations. David writes for children, young adults, and adults. Some of his other titles include *Cheese Louise*, *The Ring Bear* (an SSLI-Honor Book), and *Jacques & Spock* (a Children's Book-of-the-Month Alternate Selection). More information about David and his books can be found at **www.abdopublishing.com**.